Zach & Zoe
and the River Rescue

Zach & Zoe
and the River Rescue

by

Kristin Butcher

James Lorimer & Company Ltd., Publishers
Toronto

James Lorimer & Company Ltd., Publishers acknowledges the support of the Ontario Arts Council. We acknowledge the financial support of the Government of Canada through the Canada Book Fund for our publishing activities. We acknowledge the support of the Canada Council for the Arts for our publishing program. We acknowledge the Government of Ontario through the Ontario Media Development Corporation's Ontario Book Initiative.

The Canada Council | Le Conseil des Arts
for the Arts | du Canada

ONTARIO ARTS COUNCIL
CONSEIL DES ARTS DE L'ONTARIO

Cover design: Meredith Bangay

Library and Archives Canada Cataloguing in Publication
Butcher, Kristin
        Zach & Zoe and the river rescue / by Kristin Butcher.

(Streetlights)
Issued also in an electronic format.
ISBN 978-1-55277-707-7

        I. Title. II. Title: Zach and Zoe and the river rescue. III. Series: Streetlights

PS8553.U6972Z37 2011   jC813'.54   C2010-907326-6

James Lorimer & Company Ltd.,
Publishers
317 Adelaide Street West,
Suite 1002
Toronto, ON, Canada, M5V 1P9
www.lorimer.ca

Distributed in the
United States by:
Orca Book Publishers
P.O. Box 468
Custer, WA USA
98240-0468

Printed and bound in Canada.
Manufactured by Webcom in Toronto,
Ontario, Canada in February, 2011.
Job # 375125

MIX
Paper from
responsible sources
FSC® C004071

For my wonderful grandchildren

1

Missing

"Cock-a-doodle-doo!"

That was my sister crowing like a rooster — right into my sleeping ear. Naturally my whole body jerked awake, lifting me clear off the air mattress. I practically hit the roof of the tent.

Once my heart stopped racing and my brain figured out what had happened, I said, "What'd you do that for?"

Zoe just grinned. "It's morning. See?" Then she threw back the tent flap. Instantly spears of sunlight shot through the opening and stabbed my eyes.

"Zoe, you're blinding me!" I complained.

She let the flap fall back into place, but the grin on her face stayed right where it was. "It's time to get up."

I blinked the sleep from my eyes and squinted at the little travel clock. "Are you nuts? It's six o'clock in the morning!"

If anything, Zoe's grin got bigger. "You don't want to waste our camping trip sleeping, do you?"

I didn't, but that didn't mean I wanted to get up in the middle of the night either. But I knew there was no point trying to go back to sleep. Zoe would just impersonate a rooster again — or maybe an alarm clock. She's been my sister a long time — our whole lives actually. We're twins. So I know what she's like. Once she makes up her mind about something, that's it.

She must've woken Mom and Dad too, because I could hear groggy getting-up noises coming from their tent.

"Morning, Mom. Morning, Dad," Zoe called cheerfully.

"Says you," Mom grumbled. Her shadow fell across the wall of our tent. "We're going to be here five days, Zoe Gallagher," she muttered at the canvas. "That's plenty of time to do all the things you want to do. You will not get us up at the crack of dawn again. Do you understand?"

"Got it," Zoe beamed at Mom's shadow. "So what's for breakfast? I'm starved."

* * *

When we'd arrived at the campground the night before, it had been dark, and except for a trip down the path to the washroom we hadn't seen any of the area yet. Even though we go camping on Vancouver Island every summer, the parks are all different. So right after breakfast, Mom, Dad, Zoe, and I went on a scouting trip. We followed the narrow road that ran through the middle of the campground until we came to a *You-Are-Here* map on a wooden stand at the beginning of a winding trail.

"Fossil Footpath," Dad read. "According to the information here, the trail takes about an hour to walk and finishes down the road that way." He wagged his thumb in the direction we'd just come. "That should get us back to our campsite in plenty of time for lunch."

"Good," Mom nodded.

Zoe frowned. "What's a fossil?"

"Your father," Mom said, and then started to laugh.

Dad shot Mom a dirty look and made a big deal of clearing his throat. "A fossil, Zoe, is a rock that has a prehistoric plant or animal pressed into it. Millions of years ago, bugs and leaves sometimes fell into mud and got trapped there. Over time the mud turned to stone, and though the things trapped inside eventually disintegrated, they left impressions in the rock."

"You mean fossils are from bugs that lived way back in dinosaur times?"

"Yup. Bugs, plants — all that sort of thing."

"Zoe, don't you remember we learned about fossils at school?" I said.

She shook her head and frowned. "No, we didn't. I would've remembered. If you know about them, you probably saw it on one of those nature shows you're always watching. Anyway," she finished, "I'm going to find some of those fossils and start a collection."

"Don't set your heart on that, Zoe," Mom said. "You could be disappointed. People have been walking this trail for years. Whatever fossils were here are probably long gone."

Zoe shook her head stubbornly. "Other people couldn't have gotten all of them. There have to be some left. And I'm going to find them."

Mom knew it was a waste of time to argue with Zoe, so she just sighed and started down the trail.

It was a bright August morning, but deep in the woods you could hardly see the sky. The sun was pretty much blotted out too, except for some openings in the trees where it shone down in dusty rays that looked like they'd come from spaceships. The air was kind of cold, so I was glad I was wearing a sweatshirt.

I love being in the woods. Everything is so big, it seems to swallow you up. And there's no city noise — no traffic or construction — just quiet, so you can hear birds chirping, squirrels chattering, even snakes slithering along the ground.

There's so much to see, too — armies of bugs carrying away rotting logs, wild mushrooms growing in the underbrush, a kazillion different lichens and mosses everywhere, and birds perched in the treetops.

"Hey, Zach!" Zoe had gone on ahead and was waving madly from a rocky patch of ground off the trail. "Check this out!"

"What is it?" I called as I raced to catch up.

"Rocks."

I skidded to a stop and rolled my eyes. "What's so big about that? I've seen rocks before."

"Yeah, but these ones could have fossils in them. Help me look."

"You heard what Mom said —" I started, but then stopped because Zoe wasn't listening. She was on her hands and knees, flipping over stones. I watched as the wood bugs, earwigs, and centipedes underneath crawled off to find new homes. Zoe didn't even notice.

The thing is she hadn't picked through more than a dozen rocks before she jumped up, screaming, "I found one! I found one! I found a fossil!"

"Show me," I said skeptically. It's not that I thought Zoe was lying. It's just that she wanted to find a fossil so badly she might have imagined that she had.

She stuck the jagged piece of rock under my nose, and sure enough, there was an impression of a fern leaf in it. Zoe really had found a fossil.

Of course that meant she spent the rest of the hike turning over every stone she saw. She didn't find any more fossils, but that didn't discourage her. Even before we got back to the campsite, she was planning a return visit to the trail.

* * *

Partway through lunch, a BC Parks truck pulled into our campsite and a man in a green uniform got out. I figured he was the park ranger.

"Good afternoon, folks," he said as he walked toward the picnic table where we were sitting. "Sorry to disturb your lunch."

He looked very serious, and for a second I thought he'd found out about Zoe's fossil and had come to take it back. Zoe must've thought that too, because she stopped chewing her sandwich and put her hand on her jeans pocket where the fossil was.

"This won't take a minute," the ranger said.

Dad got up from the table. "No problem, Ranger. What can we do for you?"

The ranger handed Dad a sheet of paper. "Yesterday afternoon, a little girl went missing on the other side of the river, about five kilometres from here.

Her family was picnicking in one of the parks and she wandered off. This is her picture. She's five years old, 110 centimetres tall, and weighs eighteen kilos. Her name is Becky Lofton. She has blue eyes and shoulder-length blond hair. When last seen, she was wearing blue jeans, a pink-and-white striped t-shirt, and a pink hat."

Mom, Zoe, and I scrambled up from the table and gathered round to peer at the picture.

The little girl had a huge smile on her face. Something told me she wasn't smiling now.

The ranger continued. "Search and Rescue is looking for Becky right now. But she hasn't had any food or water since yesterday, and in this heat, we're concerned about dehydration. To make matters worse, there's a bad storm headed toward us — just a few hours away."

I looked up at the sky. There wasn't a cloud anywhere.

"Poor little thing," Mom murmured, wrapping one arm around Zoe and the other around me.

"We don't think she's wandered this way or this far," the ranger went on, "but we're asking campers to keep an eye out for her just the same. If you do see anything, please call the number at the bottom of the sheet." Then he started back toward his truck. "Thank you for your time, folks. Have a nice day."

Mom and Dad exchanged looks. Then, before I knew it, Dad was trotting after the ranger. "Could the search party use another pair of eyes?" Dad said. "I'd be happy to help out. If it were our kids lost in the woods, we'd be out of our minds with worry."

The ranger smiled and patted Dad on the shoulder. "Absolutely. Thanks. The more volunteers, the better." He pointed to the passenger door of the truck. "Hop in."

Dad glanced back at us. "I don't know exactly how long I'm going to be, but I'm sure you guys can find something to do until I get back."

2

A Discovery

"What are we going to do while Dad's gone?" I asked as Mom cleared away the lunch things.

Zoe jumped up from the table. "I know," she grinned. "Let's go back to that trail. I want to find more fossils."

I opened my mouth to protest, but Mom beat me to it. "Why don't we save that for another day? There are lots of things to do in the park, and we don't want to miss any of them." She picked up a brochure from a camping stool and started reading it. "It says here there's a trout pool on the river."

"Great!" I was suddenly excited. "Let's go fishing. We haven't done that since last summer, and I want to try out my new rod."

Mom smiled. "I know," she said. "But it's not really fair to go without your dad. He loves fishing, too."

"We can go twice. We could go today with you and then again with Dad on another day," I suggested hopefully.

Mom shook her head. "I don't think so, Zach. It's better to wait for your father."

"Can we at least check the place out?" I tried again. "We don't have to fish — just walk there to see what it's like. Where is this fishing hole anyway?"

Mom unfolded the brochure and laid it flat on the picnic table to show a map of the park. Zoe and I crowded in to see.

"There." I stabbed a finger at the map. Mom and Zoe looked where I was pointing. "Cutty Cove," Zoe read the words by my finger. "Why Cutty? Is that somebody's name?"

I shook my head. "I don't think so. Cutty is probably short for cutthroat. You know — cutthroat trout. We caught some last year. Remember?"

Zoe didn't look too sure, but she nodded. "So how far away is Cutty Cove?"

Mom studied the map for a minute and then

pointed to a bunch of tents. "Well, here's the campground," she said. "And here's the river." Her finger snaked along a wavy blue line and stopped where the river wound back on itself. "And this is Cutty Cove. I'm not great at reading maps, but from the look of things, I'd say it's about a half-hour walk. That's not too far. If your dad gets back early enough, there might still be time to go fishing today. Why don't we stick around the campsite and wait for him?"

"Aw, Mom!" Zoe groaned. "There's nothing to do here."

Mom clucked her tongue. "Of course there is."

"Like what?" Zoe demanded.

Mom shrugged. "Like read a book, maybe. There's a huge stack of books and comics in the van."

"It's summertime!" Zoe exclaimed. "I don't want to spend my holiday reading! That's what school is for. Anyway, you said the books were for in case it rains." Zoe glanced up at the sky. "And it's not."

"Fine," Mom sighed. "Why don't you play cards then — or I spy?"

"Those are also rainy day activities," I pointed out.

Mom flopped down on a camp chair and threw up

her hands. "For goodness sake, you two, stop being such wet blankets. You want to go fishing — I get that. But we're not going until your dad gets back. I don't want him walking into an empty campsite." Then her face brightened again. "I know what you can do."

"What?" Zoe and I said at the same time.

Mom smiled. "You can organize your tackle boxes and fishing gear. That way you'll be ready to go the second your dad shows up."

Zoe and I didn't argue. Organizing our gear wasn't nearly as much fun as actually fishing, but it was definitely better than reading a book or playing I spy, so we tore off to get our stuff.

Neither of us had opened our tackle boxes since last summer's camping trip, and they were a mess — like somebody had turned them upside down and shaken them. The dry flies were mixed up with the wet flies, the weights had spilled into every compartment but the one they were supposed to be in, and the leaders had gotten all tangled and knotted. It took a good half-hour to sort everything out.

After that, we decided to load up our backpacks

with the other things we might need while we were fishing. The first thing Zoe put in her pack was a roll of toilet paper.

"What are you taking that for?" I hooted.

Zoe made a face. "What do you think?" Then she looked across the campsite to a lounge chair where Mom had her nose buried in a book. "Hey, Mom," she called, "can Zach and I have a couple of apples and nutrition bars?"

Mom looked up and frowned. "You just had lunch. You can't be hungry already."

"They're not for now," Zoe said. "We want to put them in our backpacks for when we go fishing."

"Oh." Mom shrugged. "I guess so. Just make sure you fasten the latch on the cooler when you're done. We don't want any bears or raccoons helping themselves to our food."

While Zoe got the snacks, I rounded up other things — our hats and windbreakers, a pocketknife, some mosquito repellent, and antiseptic spray.

"What's the knife for?" Zoe asked when she came back with the food.

"Just in case," I said.

"In case of what?"

"In case of lots of things. Like if we need to cut our line, maybe, or dig a hook out of a tree."

Zoe's eyes instantly flashed fire. "I know what you're getting at, Zach Gallagher, and it's not funny. Just because I hooked a tree *one time* doesn't mean it's going to happen again. I can cast just as good as you."

I grinned and shoved the knife in my pack. "Says you. I think I'll take the knife anyway." Then I pointed to the mini-flashlight, compass, and binoculars she was stuffing into her bag. "Why are you taking those? It's not going to be dark, and I really don't think the compass and binoculars will help you find fish."

Zoe stuck out her tongue. "They're for exploring, smarty pants. You never know when we'll come across a hidden cave or a big hollow log or a twisty trail."

"Right." I had to work at keeping a straight face as I passed her the windbreaker and hat.

"What do we need our jackets for? It's like twenty-eight degrees."

"It could be cooler down by the river, especially if

a breeze is blowing. And you heard what the ranger said — it might rain."

"As if!" Zoe snorted. But she crammed the windbreaker into her backpack anyway.

"Now all we have to do is fill our water bottles and we're ready to go," I said. "Hey, Mom." She looked up from her book. "Zoe and I are going to the washroom to fill up our water bottles. Okay?"

She nodded. "Come right back." Then she stuck her nose in her book again.

Zoe wiggled into her backpack.

"Why are you bringing that to the washroom?" I said.

"I want to see how heavy it is — now and after we get the water. If it feels heavy walking back from the washroom, I'll take some stuff out before we go to Cutty Cove."

"Good idea" I slipped my backpack on too.

"I can't believe Mom would rather read a book than go fishing," Zoe muttered as we started down the chip trail to the washrooms.

"It's because she's a grown-up."

"Dad's a grown-up, and he likes to fish."

"Yeah, but Dad's different. I think he still wishes he was a kid."

"You should get to choose," Zoe said.

"What? Whether or not you want to grow up?"

"Yeah. I'd stay a kid for sure! What about you?"

I had to think about that. Finally I said, "I don't know. Grown-ups get to be the boss of themselves. I think I might like that."

We had arrived at a big concrete building. It was the washroom. Some campgrounds have outhouses, but this bathroom was way fancier. It had flush toilets, sinks, a water fountain, and even showers. It smelled better, too.

Zoe went in the entrance for ladies, and I went in the one for guys. The second I walked through the door I had to pee. When I was walking along the chip trail I was fine, but as soon as I got into the bathroom, I needed to go. It was weird.

Anyway, when I finished my business and went back outside, Zoe still wasn't there. Neither was anybody else. So I started looking around. Though the bathroom was pretty much surrounded by trees, a few steps farther on, the forest opened onto the river.

You had to climb down a bank to get to it, but it was right there. It was wider than I expected, and it was moving really fast, crashing into rocks that ripped it apart and hurled it into the air in ragged waves — perfect for white-water rafting. I wouldn't have wanted to try swimming in it though.

From where I was standing, I could see the washroom. I glanced over my shoulder, but there was still no sign of Zoe.

I looked back to the river. On the other side was another forested bank in every shade of green you could think of. I tried to see how many trees I knew — fir, alder, cedar, poplar, even a few arbutus.

As my eyes scanned the bank, a splotch of pink caught my eye. It reminded me of the big flower bushes in Mom's garden. But what would they be doing in the woods? They weren't wild plants.

And they didn't move!

I peered harder at the pink thing, and sure enough — it was moving. Not just waving in the breeze — which there wasn't the slightest whisper of anyway — but actually covering ground.

Little by little my eyes started picking out more

details, and though the thing kept getting blocked by the trees it passed, I caught glimpses of a face and arms and legs. This wasn't a flower bush. It was a person.

But what would somebody be doing over there? According to the park map, there were no paths in that area.

Suddenly I could hear the ranger's voice in my head:

"Yesterday afternoon, a little girl went missing on the other side of the river . . . She has blue eyes and shoulder-length blond hair. When last seen, she was wearing blue jeans, a pink-and-white striped t-shirt, and a pink hat."

I swallowed hard. Oh my gosh! I'd just found the lost little girl.

3

A Decision

I spun around to yell for Zoe and just about had a heart attack. She was standing right behind me.

"Zoe," I growled, "don't sneak up on a person like that!"

She made a face. "I didn't sneak up on you. I called your name and everything. You just didn't hear me."

There was no time to argue. I waved away Zoe's words and whirled back to the river. It took me a few seconds to pick the little girl out again. "Look!" I said, pointing in her direction. "It's the kid the park ranger told us about — the one that went missing yesterday!"

Zoe gasped. "Becky Lofton?"

I nodded. "Yeah, her."

"Where?"

"There. Straight across from us. In the woods. Look for a pink hat."

Zoe gasped again. "I see her. Oh, Zach, you found her. Beck —" she started to yell, but I quickly slammed my hand across her mouth to stop her.

"You can't call her! She might start running toward us and fall into the river!"

"Oh!" Zoe gasped. "I never even thought about that. Okay, then. You stay here and keep an eye on Becky, and I'll get Mom."

But before she could take off, I grabbed her arm.

"Wait," I said. "What's that?"

"What?"

I pointed farther along the bank. About a hundred metres behind Becky, something else was moving. "There. That black thing. Do you see it?"

Zoe squinted toward the woods. "I don't see anything but trees."

I jabbed my finger in the direction of the black thing. "You have to see it. It's right there."

"Wait a second," Zoe said as she slid her backpack to the ground and unzipped it. "Let me get the binoculars." She reached inside and pulled them out. Then she started searching the bank.

"It's a bear!" she exclaimed.

"Let me see," I said, grabbing the binoculars.

Zoe was right. It *was* a bear — a big, black one. And he was up on his hind legs.

"Why is he standing up?" Zoe said.

"He's sniffing the air."

"Why? Do you think he can smell us?"

"Not across the river."

"Can he smell Becky? Is he following her? Is he hunting her?"

"I don't think so. Black bears mostly just eat fruit and roots and fish — stuff like that. They only attack people when they are cornered or protecting their cubs." Still, this one was awfully close to Becky.

I panned the bank, looking for the pink hat. "Do you see Becky?" I asked, unable to spot her.

There was a pause as Zoe squinted into the distance. "No," she said. "I don't. Do you?"

"No." I lowered the binoculars and stared at the woods across the river as if I had X-ray vision. It didn't help. There was no pink hat and no sign of movement anywhere. "She must have wandered away from the river," I said.

"What about the bear?" There was fear in Zoe's voice.

I put the binoculars back up to my eyes, but after a few seconds I lowered them again. A chill crawled up my spine. "It's gone too."

"Oh, Zach, what if it picked up Becky's scent and went after her? And what if she got turned around and is heading back toward him? If they meet up, she could get mauled! We have to do something."

Zoe was starting to panic, and it was contagious. I told myself to stay calm. "We have to go and tell Mom what we've seen."

"There isn't time to get Mom," Zoe argued. "Becky disappeared, and now so has the bear. It could be after Becky. We have to do something *right now*."

The bear *had* disappeared — just like Becky. That was true. But it didn't mean the bear was following Becky. It had just left the river. It could be headed anywhere. That's what I told myself, anyway. Too bad I didn't believe it.

"What are you saying?" I asked, point blank.

"That you and I go and get Becky."

I waved at the rushing river. "And just how are we going to do that? We have to cross the river to get to the woods over there, and in case you haven't noticed, the water's too deep for wading and too fast for swimming."

Zoe frowned, but almost instantly her expression cleared again. "There's a bridge. I saw it on that map of the park. It's not even halfway to Cutty Cove, so it can't be more than ten minutes away — even less if we run."

"I don't know, Zoe —" I began, but she didn't let me finish.

"Think about that bear and what it could do if it caught Becky. Think about the river and how easy it would be for a tired little girl to fall into it and drown. And think how long it will take for us to get Mom and for her to contact the ranger. She'd probably have to drive to the ranger station, because cell phones don't work in the woods. Then the ranger will have to contact the search party, and they'll have to leave wherever they are now and come here. It could be hours before anybody actually starts looking for Becky!

"And it's not like they can drop down in a helicopter and pick her up, either," she continued. "They're going to have to go into the forest on foot — just like us. There might not be time for all that, Zach — especially if there's a storm. Even if the bear isn't after Becky, who knows how long until she collapses from dehydration and hunger? We have water and food. And we're here *now*. I say let's go!"

Obviously Zoe meant what she said, because she picked up her backpack and headed for the bank leading down to the river. She had made some pretty good arguments, but I still wasn't convinced. I grabbed her arm on the way by.

"What about Mom?" I said. "Eventually she's going to come looking for us, and when she doesn't find us, she is going to freak out. She's going to think we fell in the river or that we've been kidnapped or something."

"No problem," Zoe beamed. "We'll leave a trail. Watch."

Then she ran back to the bathroom, digging a trench in the chip trail with the heel of her runner. She took it to both washroom entrances, then dug a few v-shapes along it to look like arrows pointing toward the river.

"There," she said. "Now Mom will know which way we've gone, and she can follow us."

"How will she know *we* dug the trench? Anybody could've done it."

Zoe didn't hesitate for a second. "I'll leave my hat."

I shook my head. "It might blow away. Besides, you're gonna need it."

Zoe's forehead became furrowed, but not for long. "Okay. I've got another idea." She plunged her hand into her jeans pocket and pulled out the fossil she'd found that morning. "I'll leave my fossil at the end of the trench. Mom will know it's mine, and she'll know I'd never leave it behind if it weren't important. Besides, she's so wrapped up in that book she's reading, we'll probably be back before she even knows we're gone. So come on."

Without waiting for me to answer, Zoe started picking her way down the bank to the river. Obviously she was going to search for Becky with or without me. I still wasn't sure it was the right thing to do, but

I couldn't let her go alone, so I said a quick prayer that everything would work out — and Mom and Dad wouldn't kill us — and skidded down the bank after her.

Walking along the river's edge was hard; running along it was impossible. Mostly it was covered with gravel that shifted under our feet and mud that sucked our runners in like a vacuum. There were also giant boulders, trees, and exposed roots to zigzag around.

Eventually the ground became less rocky and we picked up some speed, but it was taking longer than ten minutes to get to the bridge. I was beginning to wonder if Zoe really knew where she was going. Maybe the bridge was in the other direction. But just as I was starting to give up hope, we rounded a bend and there it was.

We both started running toward it — and then slammed on the brakes.

4

Roadblock

The bridge was blocked off by a chain-link fence. A huge white sign hung in the middle of it. In giant red letters it said:

Danger! Bridge Under Repair. KEEP OUT.

For a few seconds, Zoe and I stood like statues, reading the sign over and over.

The bridge was closed. We'd come all this way for nothing. As I blinked in disbelief, Zoe suddenly took a run at the fence and threw herself onto it. It was way taller than she was, so she had to hang onto the wire and jam the toes of her runners into the holes between the chain links to keep from falling off.

"Zoe!"

I thought she was trying to climb over, so I reached out to drag her back down. But she pulled one of her feet out of its hole and began kicking behind her like a mule. So of course, I backed off.

"What are you doing?" I demanded, once I was out of range of her foot.

"I'm seeing what's wrong with the bridge," she panted, struggling to adjust her hold and find a new hole for her foot.

I cautiously inched up beside her and peered around the sign, but it was so big I couldn't see past it. "What *is* wrong with it?"

Zoe jumped down. "Not much. Some of the handrail is missing, but that's it. The rest of the bridge looks fine."

Then she whirled away and ran along the riverbank. I ran after her.

"See?" she called.

I looked where she was pointing. From this part of the bank I could see the whole bridge, and just like Zoe had said — halfway across, the handrail was gone.

"Now we *have to* go back," I said. Then I added,

"And fast. We've already wasted a bunch of time chasing down this dead-end bridge." I turned to leave, but Zoe stopped me.

"What are you talking about?" She frowned. "We can still use the bridge. It isn't broken. It just doesn't have a handrail."

"Didn't you read the sign?" I said, wagging a thumb toward the barrier. "It says KEEP OUT!"

Zoe made a face. "Of course I read the sign, but now that we know what the problem is —" she shrugged, "there is no problem. We don't need a handrail."

I think my mouth dropped open. "Are you saying you still want to cross the bridge?"

She clamped her lips together and glared at me. Then, through gritted teeth, she said, "Yes. Don't you?"

My brain was yelling *No! I don't*, but my mouth wasn't saying a thing. I looked up at the bridge. It was long and skinny. I looked down at the river racing underneath. The thought of falling into it sent a shiver up my spine.

I looked away and said, "How do you plan to get onto it?"

Zoe's face relaxed. "We could climb over the chain-link fence," she said, "but it's pretty high. I think it would be easier to get on from the bank." She pointed toward the side of the bridge. "See how the ground is built up there? If we go around the barrier to that part of the bank, we can climb onto the bridge between the rails."

I shook my head. "I don't know, Zoe."

"Well, I do," she said as she pushed past me and headed for the barrier. In one motion, she slid out of her backpack and heaved it over the fence. It landed with a thud on the floor of the bridge.

"It wouldn't fit between the rails," she explained as she started picking her way around the barrier.

I didn't like what was happening. Danger zone or not, Zoe was determined to keep going. Throwing her backpack onto the bridge pretty much proved it. So what was I supposed to do? I couldn't let her go by herself. Mom and Dad would kill me if I let Zoe get lost in the forest like that little girl. Shooting my sister a dirty look and muttering under my breath, I took off my backpack, chucked it over the fence, and headed for the bank.

Zoe was right about one thing — it *was* easy to get onto the bridge that way. At least, it was for us. A grown-up might have had some trouble crawling between the rails, but we fit no problem.

We dusted ourselves off and headed for the barrier to pick up our backpacks. As I slid my arms through the padded shoulder straps, I glanced along the rocky bank leading back to the washroom and our campsite. I think I was hoping to see Mom or Dad. Actually, I would have been happy to see any grown-up. But, except for Zoe and me, Mother Nature had the place all to herself.

I sighed and looked down the length of the bridge. There was no barricade at the other end — probably because the trail on the other side was a big circle that started and ended at the bridge. According to Mom's map, it didn't go anywhere but into the forest, and you had to cross the bridge from this side to get to it.

I turned toward Zoe. To my surprise, she was on her knees, digging through her backpack.

"Here," she said, shoving the binoculars at me. "I think we're going to need these. And this too." She handed me the silver compass and then went back to rifling through the backpack.

I stuck the compass in my pocket and slipped the strap of the binoculars over my head. "Now what are you looking for?"

She didn't even glance up. "Another clue, in case Mom comes looking for us. I want her to know which way we've gone."

"Wait a second," I said as I bent over and batted the name tag attached to the backpack strap. It was a turquoise nylon rectangle with a clear plastic front. Zoe's name and address were printed on a card inside. "What about this? We can hang it on the chain-link fence."

"Perfect!" Zoe beamed. She unhooked the tag and quickly fastened it to the fence so that it dangled over the white sign. "Mom will see that for sure. Okay," she said. "Let's go."

Walking the first half of the bridge was easy. Zoe practically ran it. Then suddenly, she stopped. As soon as I caught up to her, I knew why.

Without a railing, the rest of the bridge seemed rickety and really narrow. The river was different too — louder and closer and more ferocious. I could picture it reaching up and dragging us right off the bridge. I closed my eyes and pushed the image out of my mind.

Zoe didn't say anything. She just stood, staring at the bridge.

"Do you want to go back?" I said.

She shook her head. "We can't. We have to find Becky." But she didn't sound quite as certain as she had before.

I nodded. "Right. Well, let's do it, then." When Zoe still didn't move, I added, "Do you want me to go first?"

"Sure," she said quietly.

"Okay. But stay a few steps behind me. We don't want to bump into each other."

I needed to take a deep breath, but I figured that would make Zoe more nervous, so I gave myself a silent pep talk instead. Mind over matter. That's what Mom always says. The bridge at this end was exactly the same as it was at the other end, except it didn't have a railing. We'd walked over half the bridge already without touching the railing once, so what difference should it make?

None. That's what I told myself as I started to walk. I looked down to make sure my feet were right in the middle of the bridge. Bad idea. Out of the corner of my eye I could see the river rushing by beneath me and it made me dizzy. I quickly looked back up and focused on a tree at the end of the bridge. With each step it got a little closer, until finally it was right there. Just one more step and I was on solid ground again.

With a sigh of relief, I turned to Zoe.

But she wasn't behind me. At least not right behind me. She was still standing in the middle of the bridge. She hadn't taken a single step.

I motioned with my hand. "Come on, Zoe. Once you get going, it's easy. Just pretend the railings are there."

She took a step and then stopped. "I'm scared, Zach. What if I fall?"

"You won't," I said with more confidence than I felt. I knew exactly what Zoe was going through. "I didn't fall and neither will you. Just don't look down and you'll be fine. Look at me. Walk toward me like you were on a sidewalk."

She nodded and took a couple of steps. And then a couple more. She was doing it.

"That's it," I called to her. "You're already half-way. Just a little farther."

That was when she fell.

5

Blazing a Trail

I don't know if Zoe stepped on her shoe or her shoe-lace or if she tripped on a board. All I know is that she lost her balance and fell — not into the river, thank goodness, but flat on her face, and it scared the heck out of me.

"Zoe!" I yelled, running back onto the bridge. Suddenly it didn't matter that there wasn't a hand-rail. I knelt down beside her. "Are you okay?"

She lifted her head and stuck out her jaw. "I think I have splinters in my chin. I don't like this bridge, Zach. I want to get off. Could you drag me?"

I would've laughed if Zoe hadn't been so serious.

"No," I said, "but I think maybe we could crawl the rest of the way."

So that's what we did.

As soon as Zoe stepped off the bridge — well, crawled off, actually — all her confidence came back and she was her old self again. Except for her chin. I don't think there were any splinters in it, but she had scraped it pretty good, so we sprayed it with the antiseptic we'd brought.

At the foot of the bridge was a small clearing that led to the chip trail on the left. Unfortunately, we needed to go right to find Becky, and it was solid forest in that direction — a *huge* solid forest. We were going to have to be human bulldozers to get through it. And not get lost. And watch for the bear. And find Becky Lofton. And get back to the bridge. And then cross it again. I didn't even want to think about that part. It had been hard enough for Zoe and me to cross the bridge. What was it going to be like with a little kid?

Zoe was staring at the trees. "Up close, the forest sure is big," she murmured.

I nodded. "Yup." Then I said, "Maybe this rescue thing isn't such a good idea."

She didn't say anything. She just kept staring at the trees.

"Do you want to go back?"

She looked over her shoulder at the bridge. "Not really."

"What if we get lost? Like you said, the forest is pretty big."

"We have a compass," she reminded me. "As long as we know what direction we're supposed to be going, we'll be fine."

I shrugged. "I guess." Then I added, "But don't forget about the bear. It's somewhere in the forest too."

"I haven't forgotten," she replied. "That's one of the reasons I think we should keep going. Becky has no one to protect her."

"That's true. So you really think we should do this?"

"Yes."

"You're not just saying that because you don't want to go back over the bridge? You'll have to cross it again sometime, you know."

"You don't have to remind me," Zoe snapped.

"Sorry," I said. And I was. I hadn't meant to make her feel bad.

"Right." She faked a smile and turned away from

the river. "Okay, we're going to find Becky." she sounded positive again. "So let's go."

Zoe tramped over to the chip trail, and using the heel of her runner — just like she'd done at the washroom — she drew a big X. Then she drew an arrow pointing toward the forest we were about to enter. Finally, she wrote "Z & Z" beside it.

"There," she said. "I think that should do it. Don't you?" She didn't wait for me to answer. "That'll tell Mom which way we've gone."

"Well, if your drawing doesn't send her in the right direction, the trail of bushes we're going to trample sure will."

We both looked at the solid wall of forest and Zoe stretched her arm toward it. "After you," she said.

"Yeah, right!" I snorted. "You always want to go first, but suddenly you want *me* to lead the way. Hmmm, I wonder why." I shook my head and plowed into the woods.

At least, I *tried* to plow into the woods. But it was like the forest had put up a force field. Huge trees were staggered like giant watchman every two or three metres. Overlapping thorny bushes filled the gaps in between. There was no easy way in.

I stuck my arms out in front of me and started to walk. Zoe was right behind. The branches scraped and cracked, and snapped off, pinging our faces. Thorns and prickly leaves snagged our clothes and tore at our arms and hands.

"Ow! Ow, ow, ow!" I winced, pulling away from the clawing bushes so fast I smacked right into Zoe, and we both tumbled backwards onto the ground.

I rubbed my arms. There were big red welts all over them.

"This is no good," I said. "We're going to get cut to shreds."

I shrugged off my backpack and dug around inside for my jacket and hat. When Zoe saw what I was doing, she put her windbreaker and hat on too.

"Hopefully, this will help," I said as I plunged into the forest for the second time.

We still got scratched, but it was way better, and after about ten steps we broke through into a clear space — well, sort of a clear space. There were still trees and giant ferns everywhere, but not nearly so many bushes, which meant we could walk around

47

them without getting attacked.

Though the river was mostly hidden by the forest, we could still hear it, so I knew it was on our right — and that's exactly where I wanted to keep it. My plan was to follow it until we picked up Becky's trail.

I pulled the compass out of my pocket and flipped open the cover. The needle bounced back and forth for a few seconds until it found north. I turned the compass so that the directional symbol lined up with the needle. We were headed east.

I wondered what time it was. I don't wear a watch and neither does Zoe, so I had to guess. Considering where the sun was and how long we'd been on the move, I figured it was probably somewhere around two o'clock — maybe a little later.

I wondered where Dad and the other searchers were. Were they on Becky's trail, too? As we got farther away from the bridge, it made me feel a little better to think they might be closing in on us from another direction.

"Maybe we should leave another clue," I said to Zoe. "We aren't going to be trampling any more bushes — at least not for a while — so we need to let

Mom know which direction we're headed."

"Good idea," Zoe agreed, as she glanced around for something to use.

There was no chip trail here for her to draw a picture in with her shoe. The forest floor was hard-packed earth and evergreen needles.

"How about tying something to one of these bushes? A little farther on we can do it again, and then maybe one more time after that. That way if Mom or the search party comes across our trail, they'll know we're headed east."

Zoe nodded and started digging through her backpack. She pulled out the roll of toilet paper and held it up. "There's this. I could poke pieces of it onto the bushes. The white will really show up against the green."

"That would be good," I said, and then remembering a storm was headed our way, I added, "as long as it doesn't rain."

We wrapped the toilet paper onto the bushes and kept going. We were making pretty good time. I figured the bridge was about two kilometres from where we'd first seen Becky. We'd probably covered about half that distance so far. It was time to start looking for her trail.

It was beginning to get really warm. We were sweating so much, our clothes were sticking to us. So we took off our jackets and tied them around our waists. Bad idea. As soon as we pushed the next tree bough out of the way, every mosquito in the forest showed up. It was like we'd invited them to lunch — and we were the food! We were in a cloud of mini-vampires. We didn't have enough hands to smack them all, and we were dancing and twirling and ducking at warp speed, just trying to get out of the way.

"Do something!" Zoe squealed, batting at herself and the air. "I'm getting eaten alive!" As she tried to spin away, she snagged her foot on a big tree root and — for the second time that day — went sprawling. "Help, Zach!" she cried, hopping back up.

"Put your jacket on," I hollered, as I struggled into my own. "I'll find the insect repellent."

It was all I could do to slip off my backpack and unzip it. Mosquitoes were buzzing in my ears and flying up my nose. They were even trying to land on my eyelids. Finally I found the can of repellent. There was no time to shake it, so I just snapped off the lid and started spraying — first the air and then me.

"Shut your eyes and stand still," I told Zoe, as I sprayed her from head to foot.

She started to cough and backed away to find some fresh air. "Acchh! That stuff smells awful." She made a face and waved wildly at the air.

"It gets rid of the mosquitoes, though," I pointed out.

"For now," she grumbled, glancing nervously around her. "Let's get moving before they come back." She put out her hand. "I'll carry the insect repellent."

After a while, we spotted a clearing about a hundred metres away. I lifted the binoculars for a better look.

It was kind of weird to see a meadow right in the middle of the woods with the sun beaming down on it. Just sunshine and green grass — that was all. It was like an oasis in the dark forest.

I passed the binoculars to Zoe.

"Cool," she said. "Maybe Becky's there."

I shook my head. "I don't think so. She was already past this spot when we saw her across the river — and she was walking away from the clearing, not toward it. I think she's still ahead of us."

"Maybe," Zoe conceded as she looked through the binoculars. "Hey, Zach, did you see those black-berry bushes?"

I hadn't.

As she passed back the binoculars, Zoe swiped at her forehead with her arm. Her hair was damp and stuck to her head and her face shone with sweat. Streaks of dirt smeared her cheeks. She looked hot and tired. I knew the feeling.

I panned the clearing again. I don't know why I hadn't seen the blackberry bushes before; they were pretty obvious — running like a hedge all around the edge of the clearing. I zoomed in on the fat, juicy ber-ries, and my mouth started to water. "Okay," I said, "let's head there. We could both use a rest. Let's take a five minute break, have a drink of water, eat some berries, and then decide which way to go next."

Though we were both exhausted, the thought of those berries energized us and we picked up speed. Not even the gnats swarming around our heads could slow us down.

It was a loud rustling sound that made us freeze in our tracks.

"What was that?" Zoe mouthed the words.

I looked up into the trees, thinking the wind might be blowing the leaves, but there wasn't a hint of a breeze.

I listened hard. There was the rustling again. The sound seemed to be coming from the clearing.

"Maybe it *is* Becky," I whispered. "Maybe she wandered back this way."

Zoe gasped and pointed straight ahead. "I don't think so," she squeaked.

6

Unwelcome Company

I looked toward the clearing, and there was a black bear lumbering across the grass. It couldn't have been more than twenty steps away. My heart leaped into my mouth, and my stomach started doing somersaults.

Zoe latched onto my arm. "What are we going to do?" Her voice was barely there, but I could tell she was scared.

"Don't panic," I said to myself as much as to her.

But it was like she didn't hear me. She started yanking on my arm. "Come on, Zach. We have to get out of here before the bear sees us."

"Don't panic!" I repeated in a low growl that I hoped sounded confident, even though my feet and legs were all set to do exactly what Zoe was suggesting. "If we move too fast the bear will notice, and we don't want that. We have to stay calm and try to remember what we know about bears."

"We know they're big," Zoe whispered.

The bear *was* pretty big. Not as big as a grizzly, but a good size for a black bear. It probably weighed twice as much as my dad did.

"And they have sharp claws and teeth," Zoe continued.

I looked down at my own clipped fingernails and ran my tongue over my teeth. They were pretty pathetic weapons compared to what the bear had. If it came down to a battle, we wouldn't stand a chance.

The bear headed for the far side of the clearing. While his back was to us, I grabbed Zoe's arm and started walking toward a nearby bush.

"Move really slow," I said in a quiet voice.

As we ducked behind the bush, Zoe said, "Can the bear see this far?"

"If we can see it, it can probably see us. It just doesn't know to look. Besides, bears trust their noses more than their eyes."

"Do you think it can smell us?"

"I don't know . . . I don't think so," I said. "But if a wind comes up and starts blowing behind us, it'll carry our scent right to him. Cross your fingers that doesn't happen. We don't want the bear to know we're here."

Zoe's eyes opened really wide.

"It's probably nothing to worry about. There hasn't been a breeze all day," I added quickly. "If we stay still and quiet, I think we'll be okay. The bear just wants to eat some berries. When it's had enough, it'll leave, and then we can go."

But until that happened, all we could do was wait. So that's what we did. After a while we weren't even that scared, because it felt like we were watching a wildlife documentary on television. The only difference was that this was real life — and there was no popcorn.

Zoe and I took turns looking through the binoculars, watching where the bear went and waiting for the chance to get away.

The bear was a male. I could tell by his size and also by the fact that he was on his own. Female bears are a lot smaller and usually have cubs with them in the summertime. Male bears only hang out with other bears when it's mating season. The rest of the time they wander around on their own.

The bear worked his way along the back of the clearing and then started eating his way down the side, sticking his snout right into the bushes. Blackberry bushes are full of thorns, but that didn't seem to bother the bear. Then, for no reason that I could tell, he stopped, lifted his nose in the air, and started sniffing. But I guess he wasn't picking up enough that way, because after a few seconds of that, he stood up and sniffed.

Holy macaroni! It felt like he was staring straight at Zoe and me. We huddled closer together and made ourselves as small as we could. Finally the bear got down on all fours again and started walking to the front of the clearing — right toward us!

"He sees us. He knows we're here," Zoe squeaked.

"Shhhh," I hushed her. My heart was racing.

At the front of the clearing, the bear stood up again.

Zoe gasped, and I stopped breathing. That close

and up on his hind legs, the bear was enormous — as tall as my dad. Even without the binoculars, I could see his huge, clawed paws. He could take us both out with one swat.

Though he was looking in our direction, he didn't seem to know we were there. Dad said black bears are actually timid and would rather run away from humans than confront them.

I sure hoped he was right.

The bear dropped down again and padded over to a tree. He gave it a good sniff, then reared back up on his hind legs and grabbed it. The bark cracked and splintered as he scraped his claws down the tree again and again. Then he wrapped his front legs right around the trunk and started rubbing his big body against it.

"He's scratching himself," Zoe whispered. "He must have an itch."

A really *big* itch! He used the tree as a scratching post for at least five minutes. He scratched his belly, his sides — even his head and neck.

Eventually he let go and wandered back to the blackberry bushes. But he seemed to have lost interest, and after just a couple of mouthfuls, he turned away and headed out of the clearing the way he'd come.

Zoe and I heaved a sigh of relief at the same moment. Then I turned to her and we both smiled nervously. The bear might be gone, but that didn't mean we were out of danger. With all those black-berries still to be eaten, he probably wouldn't wander far. It was almost more scary not being able to see him, because I kept wondering where he was. What if he was doubling back to sneak up on us from behind? I decided not to share that thought with Zoe.

We stayed crouched behind the bush for a while longer, but the bear never came back.

Finally I said, "I think it's safe to go. The bear is gone."

"Are you sure?" Zoe was still whispering.

"No, not completely," I confessed in my normal voice and stood up. "Just in case, let's not go through the clearing. Let's walk around the outside of it in-stead. It'll take longer, but it'll be safer. The bear went left, so we'll go right."

"Good idea," Zoe said as she got to her feet. She handed me a few pieces of toilet paper. "Let's mark some bushes so we leave a trail."

I nodded and started walking. The sooner we found Becky and got out of the forest, the happier I'd be.

At first we tried to stay really quiet — just in case the bear was still hanging around. As we rounded the end of the clearing, we peered anxiously through the gaps in the bushes, looking for a big splotch of black. Not that we wanted to see one, but we didn't want to get caught by surprise either.

Once we were past the clearing, the trees and bushes became really thick again. It was even darker in this part of the forest. There were huge ferns, fallen trees, and giant exposed roots. And there was moss everywhere. It coated the tree trunks and even dripped from the branches. A single path snaked through the middle, so we followed it. If Becky had come this way, I was pretty sure she would have taken the path too.

I checked the compass. We were heading north. As soon as the forest let us, we were going to have to start heading east again.

"These bushes and roots can't go on forever," I

said to Zoe. "Keep your eyes open for a way through."

"Right."

We continued for a few more minutes without seeing anything. Then suddenly, the path ended. There was nowhere else to go. My heart dropped into my stomach. What were we supposed to do now?

Zoe pointed to the thorny hedge beside us.

"Look!" she exclaimed. "It's a hole."

"Where?" A spark of hope flared inside me.

"Right there. Down low. It looks like it might be some sort of animal tunnel."

I got down on my hands and knees and stared into it.

"It's pretty dark in there. And twisty. I can't see where it comes out."

Zoe crouched down beside me and after a good, long look, she got on all fours and started in.

"Wait a second." I grabbed onto her. "What if it's a dead end?"

She shook away my hand. "What other choice do we have?" Then she started moving again.

She was right. There was nowhere else to go, so I tied a piece of toilet paper to the bush above the opening and headed in after her.

The hole was just big enough for us to crawl through. The ground was hard and smelled damp and earthy. Fir needles jabbed the palms of my hands and twigs clawed at my jacket and backpack.

"I can see the other side," Zoe said over her shoulder. "We're just about there."

"Good," I grumbled. "My knees are killing me."

When I finally reached the end of the tunnel, it felt so good to stand up and stretch my legs and my back. I took a deep breath. It felt good to stretch my lungs, too. I turned around to look at where we'd been. What I saw made my heart skip a beat.

"Zoe," I said. "Look!"

She spun around. "Is that —"

I nodded and freed the pink hat from the branch it was snagged on. Then I passed it to Zoe. I couldn't help smiling. "I think we've found Becky's trail."

7

Following the Trail

Becky Lofton had crawled through the hole in the hedge. The pink hat proved it. We'd found her trail. Now all we had to do was follow it.

We glanced around. This part of the forest looked exactly like the part on the other side of the prickly hedge — giant trees, scratchy bushes, and moss everywhere.

I figured Becky would have taken the easiest route, and that was a path leading right. Unless my sense of direction had gotten all mixed up while we were crawling through the hole, that meant the path should take us back to the river. A quick check of the compass said I was right.

We studied the ground for more clues — footprints

or anything Becky might have dropped. But there was nothing. The ground was thick with decaying leaves, cedar boughs, and fir needles, but no footprints, and there wasn't a tissue or candy wrapper anywhere. The hat told us she'd crawled through the hole, but it didn't tell us where she'd gone after that. All we could hope was that she'd stayed on the path.

As Zoe tied another piece of toilet paper onto a bush, I peered back into the hole.

"What're you doing?" she asked.

"Looking."

"For what?"

I shrugged. "I want to see how big the tunnel is."

"Why?" Zoe made a face. "It was big enough for Becky to crawl through and for you and me to crawl through after her."

I frowned. "Yeah. But is it big enough for a rescuer to crawl through?"

There was a pause before Zoe said, "Oh. I hadn't thought about that."

Though we'd been leaving regular clues for the search party, we hadn't actually talked about anyone following us since we'd crossed the bridge. But that didn't stop me from looking back every few minutes, hoping someone would be there. And it didn't stop me from straining my ears for the sound of voices.

Zoe came over to me and put a hand on my shoulder. "They'll come," she said.

I nodded. "Yeah, I know." I just wished they'd come now. I didn't want to have to act grown up anymore. I wanted to go back to being a kid.

A flutter of panic zipped through me. Right now, Zoe and I were supposed to be standing on the bank of a fishing hole with Dad, casting our lines for trout. The biggest worry we should've had was whether or not we'd catch a fish. But instead, we were in the middle of a huge forest, trying to find a little girl without getting lost ourselves. For all I knew, we already were.

Zoe must have read my mind. She can do that sometimes. I guess it's because we're twins. "We're going to be fine," she said. "We've found Becky's trail, and pretty soon we'll find her. Then we'll head back. We'll be like Hansel and Gretel, except we'll be following toilet paper instead of bread crumbs."

She had such a goofy grin on her face that I couldn't help smiling too.

"Along the way, Dad and the search party will catch up to us and we'll all go home together and live happily ever after," she finished.

I glanced at the hole.

"You don't need to worry about that, either," she told me cheerfully. "Either we'll crawl back through it on our way out of the forest, or Dad will chop it down like Paul Bunyan."

"I think you're getting your fairy tales mixed up," I said.

Zoe shrugged. "Whatever. Are you ready?"

I took a deep breath and nodded. "Yup. Let's go."

Zoe can bug me sometimes, but at that moment I was really glad she was with me. Maybe she wasn't thinking about all the stuff that could go wrong, or maybe she was just braver than I was. It didn't matter. The fact that she was acting exactly like she always acts settled my nerves right down and made me believe that everything was going to be fine.

"Hey, maybe we'll get a reward for finding Becky," Zoe said, as we tramped along the trail. "That would be cool."

"Zoe!"

"Don't sound so shocked," she said. "It *would* be cool, and you know it. I wonder how big a reward it would be."

"Zoe!" I exclaimed again.

It was like she didn't even hear me. "I bet you anything we'll be on television, too. And in the newspaper. We'll have reporters chasing us down all over the place for pictures and interviews. We'll be heroes. We might even get a medal. I've seen programs like that on television, where kids who do brave deeds get medals. If we did, I'd —"

And that's when she walked into me.

"Do you mind?" I complained.

"Sorry," she said. "Why did you stop?"

"I had to," I grumbled. "There's no more path. If you weren't so busy daydreaming, you would have noticed that too."

She peered around me. "Oh. You're right. So now what?"

"So now we have to figure out which way Becky went from here."

We both started looking around. We were surrounded by rotting logs, giant trees, and prickly bushes.

"Come over here," Zoe called from down the path. She'd backtracked, looking for a clue. "There's a tiny space between this big tree stump and these bushes — just the right size for a little kid to squeeze through. I can see some broken twigs, too. I think this is the way Becky went."

I went to look.

"You might be right," I said. "Anyway, it's worth a try."

After leaving another toilet-paper clue, we squeezed through the skinny opening. On the other side was a path so narrow that bushes and branches snagged us as we walked past. The path twisted back and forth, but we kept following it. The trees weren't quite as big in this part of the forest, so more sunlight got through, which meant there were a lot more plants on the ground for us to trip over. Zoe and I spent so much time watching where we were putting our feet that I got hit in the face with a branch of spit-bug gob, and Zoe ran into a sticky spiderweb.

Eventually we came to a place where the path split. One part continued straight ahead, while the other veered off.

"Let's go right," I said, as I tied toilet paper to a bush. "That'll take us toward the river. Keep a lookout for Becky. She has to be around here somewhere."

The path we were on now was every bit as twisty as the one we'd just left, and after a while I couldn't tell which direction we were going. All I knew was that we were getting deeper and deeper into the forest.

But there was still no sign of Becky.

"Maybe we should call her name," Zoe suggested. "If she's around here, she'll hear us."

"Good idea," I said.

Not only would it help us find Becky, it would also help the rescuers find us. If they were close enough to hear us yelling, they'd be there in a minute. And if the bear heard us, our shouting would probably scare him off.

"Becky! Becky Lofton! Becky, where are you?" we called as we walked.

Then we stopped and listened. But there was no answer.

That worried me a little, because I figured we should have caught up with Becky by now.

After a while, Zoe tugged on my jacket. "Hey,

Zach. Look over there."

"Where? What? Do you see Becky?"

"No," Zoe said. "I see a piece of toilet paper tied to a bush. We're back where the two paths meet."

"No," I groaned, letting my legs collapse beneath me. I sank to the ground like a rock. "You mean we've spent this whole time walking in a circle?" I groaned again.

"Looks that way." Zoe dropped down beside me. "So now what do we do?"

I squinted up through the trees, trying to find the sun. It was hidden behind angry clouds. "It looks like the ranger was right," I said. "There is a storm coming. We have to find Becky and get out of here before it hits."

"How long do you think we have?" Zoe asked.

"I don't know — but not long."

"What time is it now?"

"Five or six o'clock," I said.

"Suppertime."

As if to prove Zoe was right, my stomach growled.

"Mmmm," Zoe sighed. "I could use a big fat hamburger and corn on the cob right now, and maybe blackberry pie with ice cream for dessert."

My stomach growled again.

"Cut that out, Zoe," I said. "You're making me hungry."

"I'm hungry too," said a little voice behind us.

Zoe and I both spun toward the sound, but all we saw was a fir tree with big, droopy branches.

Zoe blinked. "Did that tree just say it was hungry?"

Near the ground a branch moved and a little blond head poked out beneath it. "That's silly," it said. "Trees can't talk."

8

Found

"Are you Becky?" Zoe and I said at the same time. I guess it was kind of a stupid question. I mean what other five-year-old kids were wandering around in the forest?

Becky frowned. "Are you strangers? I'm not supposed to talk to strangers."

Zoe shook her head. "No, we're not." She pointed to me. "That's Zach. And I'm Zoe. And we've brought your hat. You lost it."

Becky touched her head. "Where is it?"

Zoe pulled the hat out of her backpack. "Here."

Becky put it on. "I'm thirsty. I'm hungry. I'm itchy. I want to go home. I —" That's when the world fell apart. "I want my mommy!"

Suddenly Becky was crying and screaming at the top of her lungs. And for a few very long minutes I wished my ears would fall off.

"Don't cry, Becky. Don't cry. It's all right. Everything is going to be okay," Zoe said in a soothing voice. She reached a hand out to the little girl, but Becky pushed it away and cried harder.

Zoe shoved her backpack toward me. "Get some water and one of those nutrition bars," she said quietly. "I'll try to calm Becky down."

I nodded and began digging around in the backpacks.

"It's okay, Becky," Zoe said again. "Zach and I are going to take you to your mommy."

Instantly the crying stopped. I was so surprised, I turned to see if Becky was all right. She seemed to be. In fact, she looked pretty much the same as she had a few minutes ago. The only difference was that I couldn't see her tonsils anymore and she wasn't wailing like a police siren. Her cheeks were smeared with tears and dirt, and she was breathing in short little hiccups, but the look on her face had gone from scared to curious.

"You know where my mommy is?" she said in a small voice. "I lost her."

Zoe nodded reassuringly. "Well, she's not lost anymore, and we're going to take you to her. Would you like that?"

Becky's mouth quivered, but she nodded. "Yes, please." Then she blinked, sending another fat tear tumbling down her cheek.

"Okay, then," Zoe smiled. "First we have to get you away from that tree." She helped Becky crawl out of her hiding place.

She was all rumpled and dirty. She'd lost one of her pigtails, and the hair on that side of her head was tangled and full of pine needles. Her nose was sunburned, and her arms were covered in scratches and bug bites. But other than that, she looked okay.

"How'd you get under that tree anyway?" Zoe asked.

Becky shrugged. "I was hot and tired. It was cool under the tree. So I rolled under it and went to sleep. Then I heard you guys talking and I woke up."

"You are a very brave girl," Zoe said.

I screwed the cap off the water bottle. "Here's

some water, Becky. I know you're thirsty, but don't gulp it, or it'll make you sick. Just take a little sip, swish it around in your mouth, and swallow it. Then you can have some more. Understand?"

She nodded, but when I handed her the bottle, she started guzzling, and I quickly grabbed it away. Of course, that set her howling again.

"I want water!" she cried and stomped her foot. "Give it to me."

I didn't want her to have another meltdown, so I kept my voice really calm. "You can have some more in a minute. I promise. But first you have to let your tummy get used to the water you just drank."

She stomped her foot again and shot daggers at me with her eyes. "I want the water *now*!" Then she lunged for the bottle.

Though I hadn't expected to be attacked, it was no big deal to hold the bottle out of Becky's reach. Unfortunately, avoiding her kicks and punches wasn't quite as easy.

Zoe stared at us with her mouth hanging open. I shot her a pleading look. "Hello? I could use a little help here."

That brought her back to life. "Right," she said, grabbing Becky around the waist from behind and dragging her away.

Since I was now out of reach, Becky started swinging at Zoe. She hit her in the head with her elbows and hacked at her shins with her heels. For somebody who hadn't eaten in over a day, she had a lot of energy.

"Ow, ow, ow!" Zoe winced, and then — still hanging onto Becky — she spun toward a tree. "Becky Lofton, stop hitting me right this second, or I'm going to throw you back under the tree. I mean it!"

To my surprise, Becky stopped thrashing around. "Put me down," she pouted.

"Pardon me?" Zoe replied in a voice that was every bit as unfriendly as the little girl's. "I think you forgot the magic word."

Zoe is the Queen of Bossy, so I'm used to her telling *me* what to do. But this was a five-year-old kid she was ordering around. The thing is, I could tell she meant business. She sounded just like Mom. I was impressed.

I don't know if Becky was, though. She didn't

seem in a hurry to do what Zoe said. She just got stiff as a board and glared into space.

I could hear Zoe puffing as she waited for Becky to answer. She'd been holding the little girl for a couple of minutes already, and I guess she was getting tired. I thought about helping her out, but I was afraid Becky would turn on me again. Besides, this was a showdown. It was a willful five-year-old against a stubborn ten-year-old, and I wanted to see who would win.

I really hoped it was Zoe.

"Well?" Zoe panted. "This is your last chance, Becky. Say the magic word and I'll put you down. If you don't, I'm sticking you back under the tree and leaving you there."

I think it was the last part of the threat that got to Becky. "Put me down," she blurted and then added more meekly, "please."

As Zoe set the little girl on the ground, my muscles tensed, getting ready for another attack.

But it didn't happen. Becky didn't apologize or anything — little kids never do that unless they're forced — but suddenly it was like she had never thrown a fit. She was totally polite and even smiled when she said, "Could I have some more water, please, Zach?"

I couldn't believe my eyes and ears. It was like flipping a switch — one second the kid was a monster and the next she was sweet as pie.

I gave her back the bottle, and this time she drank the water slowly. Then we gave her a few pieces of the nutrition bar and put antiseptic on all her cuts and scratches. Even though she was already covered in bug bites, we sprayed her arms and legs with insect repellent in case the mosquitoes showed up again.

We were ready to begin the return trip. I figured it would be a lot easier and faster, because we weren't blazing a trail anymore — we were following one. We had all those toilet paper signposts to show us the way back. Soon this whole rescue thing would be behind us. And that was just fine with me.

As we shrugged on our backpacks, I squinted at the sky. "If we really move, I think we can make it out of the forest before dark."

Zoe nodded. "Okay, let's do it."

Unfortunately, Becky wasn't quite as cooperative.

For a little kid, she'd done really well in the forest on her own, but now she was tired and cranky and hungry and thirsty, and she didn't understand how important it was to hurry.

"Come on, Becky," I called for the hundredth time. "We have to keep going."

She scowled at me from the middle of the path where she had thrown herself down.

"You want to get home, don't you?" Zoe tried to coax her back onto her feet. "You want to see your mommy, right?"

Tears welled up in Becky's eyes. The kid could turn on the waterworks in a second.

I sighed and stared up into the trees. At the rate we were going, we were never going to get out of the forest.

Even after Becky got moving again, our progress was slow. A snail could've made better time. If Becky wasn't dragging her feet or plunking herself on the ground, she was complaining. I know it sounds mean, but I almost wished we'd never found her. Zoe was the patient one, and somehow she kept finding ways to urge Becky on.

When I spotted the clearing through the binoculars, I felt more lighthearted than I had all day.

Until I saw the bear.

I hadn't thought he would go far. And I was right. Darn those blackberries!

If the bear was still hanging around, we couldn't take the shortcut through the clearing. We weren't going to be able to walk around the end like we had before, either. We were going to have to circle around the bear and blaze a new trail in a totally different direction. Suddenly I wasn't so sure we were going to make it out of the forest before dark. My heart sank.

At the same time I could hear an annoying little voice at the back of my thoughts. It was Becky. She had been whining practically non-stop since we'd found her. That didn't help calm my nerves. I didn't even want to think what the bear would do if he heard her.

I turned to Zoe and whispered anxiously, "The bear is back. You've got to keep Becky quiet."

Zoe nodded. "Give me the binoculars."

She scanned the clearing for the bear. Then she knelt down beside Becky.

"Becky," she whispered, "we have to be very, very quiet. We're close to a bear. If we make noise, he'll hear us, and that wouldn't be good. The bear could hurt us. Do you understand?"

Becky crossed her arms over her chest and stuck out her chin. "I don't believe you. You're just saying that so I won't talk."

Zoe shook her head. "No, I'm not. Look." Through the binoculars, she showed Becky the bear.

Becky pushed the binoculars away and grabbed onto Zoe.

"Don't let it eat me!" she cried.

"Shhh!" Zoe and I hushed her at the same time.

"The bear isn't going to eat you," I said. "He doesn't know we're here, and we're going to leave before he notices. We're going to take a long walk around him. I'll go first. You'll follow me. Zoe will follow you. But you have to be quiet as a mouse. Can you do that?"

Wide-eyed with fear, Becky nodded.

"Good girl," I said. "Let's go."

9

Lost!

My plan was to circle the clearing and join up with our trail on the other side. It would take more time, but if we hurried, we might still make it back to the bridge before dark. That's what I hoped, anyway.

Too bad that's not how things worked out.

The entire forest had been tough to walk through, but the part we were in now was nearly impossible. The ground went up hills and into gullies, and there were boulders and fallen trees everywhere. It was like a giant had scooped up a handful of the woods and thrown it down again. It was one big, tangled mess.

For the first while we headed north — away from the river and the clearing. I wanted to get us as far from the bear as I could. When I thought we'd put enough distance between us and him, I turned west. At least, I tried to turn west, but it was like the forest wouldn't let me. I kept running into dead ends — logs that were too big or slippery with moss to climb over, enormous boulders, giant tree roots, even a few deep holes. All we could do was zigzag around the obstacles. One minute we were headed west, the next we were going south, then east, then south again. I was checking the compass constantly. Not that it helped. We'd made so many detours, I had no idea where the clearing was anymore. For all I knew we were walking straight back toward the bear.

We didn't talk. Not even Becky. She didn't make a peep. No tears, no tantrums — nothing. The idea of getting eaten by the bear had scared her quiet.

I started to feel sorry for her. After all, she *was* only five, and she was little. She'd already spent a night in the forest — *alone* — and now she was being ordered around by two kids she didn't even know. All she'd had to eat and drink in the last day and a half was what Zoe and I had given her, and that wasn't very much. If I was tired from marching through the forest — which I was — Becky had to be exhausted.

As if to prove it, she stumbled and fell. She started to cry. She clapped her hands over her mouth to hold in the sound, but her shoulders shook with each unhappy sob.

Zoe crouched down and hugged her. "It's okay, Becky. Don't cry," she said as she rubbed the little girl's back. Then she looked at me. "She needs to rest, Zach. I know we have to get out of the forest, but Becky can't keep going. I've been watching her. She can barely lift her feet."

I looked up through the trees. It was solid gray clouds now, and a breeze had started to blow. Night was coming on — and so was the storm.

If I'd thought we were close to the bridge, I'd have pushed Becky to keep going. Heck, I would have piggybacked her myself. But that was the thing. I didn't know where we were. Nothing looked familiar, and we hadn't come across any bushes trimmed with toilet paper to show us the way. There was no point pushing Becky if we weren't near where we needed to be.

I reached into my jacket pocket for the compass, but all I got was lint. I tried the other pocket. The compass wasn't there, either. And it wasn't in my jeans. I checked my pockets again. I even considered tearing my backpack apart, but I hadn't had it off since we'd seen the bear. I knew it wasn't going to be in there.

I frowned.

"What's the matter?" Zoe said.

"I can't find the compass. Did I give it to you?"

She shook her head.

"Check your pockets."

But Zoe didn't have it either.

"I must have dropped it," I said. "Great! Without the compass we're toast."

"We could look for it," Zoe suggested.

"What's the point?" I barked at her. I was tired and frustrated, just like Becky. "This forest is one big maze. We won't find it. It's gone — lost." I didn't add *and so are we*, but I was sure thinking it.

Zoe refused to get discouraged. "Then we'll just have to find our way back using the sun," she said.

I pointed to the sky. "Except the sun is gone. There's nothing but clouds, and soon it'll be dark."

There was a long pause as we thought about the situation.

Then Becky whimpered, "I'm hungry. I'm thirsty. I'm tired."

Zoe and I both knew what came after that, and neither of us had the strength for another one of Becky's meltdowns.

"We're going to have something to eat right away," Zoe said quickly. "Aren't we, Zach?"

"Absolutely," I nodded. "We're going to set up camp, have something to eat, and then go to sleep. And when we wake up in the morning, we're going to walk out of the forest and go home. Does that sound good?"

I held my breath as I waited for Becky's answer. Would it be a screaming fit or . . .

She nodded and rested her head against Zoe. I started to breathe again, but my stomach was getting tighter and tighter.

Daylight was fading, and a storm was coming. There was a bear on the loose — probably somewhere nearby. We were definitely lost, and all we had in the way of food was one measly nutrition bar and two apples. Our water was running low, too. It was not a good situation, and I could feel myself starting to panic.

But Zoe and Becky were counting on me to get us out of this mess. I had to stay calm. I had to think. I took a deep breath and tried to squash my fear.

"You and Becky stay here," I said. "I'm going to scout around for a place to spend the night. I'll stay within shouting distance so I don't get lost." I thought about what I'd just said and almost laughed. How could I get more lost than I already was?

Zoe nodded, but she looked worried. "Okay, but don't be too long. We have to stay together." Then she dug into her jacket pocket and pulled out the dwindling roll of toilet paper. "Here," she said as she pressed it into my hand, "Mark your trail — just in case."

I shoved the roll into my pocket. Then I dropped my backpack onto the ground. It was just extra weight. "Wish me luck," I said and trudged off.

As the girls disappeared from sight I suddenly felt very alone, and once again, panic threatened to swamp me. *Don't feel. Just think!* I scolded myself.

What should I be looking for? A clearing would be best. It would be easier for searchers to see us there. But we still needed a place that was sheltered. When the storm hit, it could get ugly. A big tree with wide boughs would give us some protection.

After about ten minutes of poking around, I came to a patch of bare ground with a big cedar tree on one side. It wasn't a big space, but it would do.

"Zoe!" I shouted.

"Zach?" she hollered back. She didn't sound too far away.

"I've found a place. I'm coming back now."

When I rounded a curve in the path, I saw Zoe and Becky waiting for me. The light was leaking out of the day fast. I pulled on my backpack and led them to the clearing.

The most important thing was to get a bed ready before the light was gone. Dad had told us never to lie right on the ground. It was damp and cold, and would suck away our body heat. Sawing boughs and skinny branches from the trees with the knife I'd packed, Zoe and I quickly stacked them under the cedar tree. When we were done, we had a platform about as thick as a mattress and just about as soft. We plugged the holes with clumps of moss.

"There," Zoe announced. "Now we have somewhere to sleep." Then she glanced toward Becky.

"Aw," she said softly.

I turned to look. Becky was huddled between the two backpacks, struggling to stay awake.

Zoe clapped her hands. "Time for supper."

Becky's eyes fluttered open. "Supper?"

"Uh-huh," Zoe nodded. She opened the backpacks and hauled out the water bottles. One was half full; the other had only a couple of mouthfuls left. She twisted off the cap of that one and passed it to Becky. "Drink it slowly," she said. "And whatever you do, don't spill."

Becky did as she was told. I think she was too tired to rebel.

Since Becky had eaten one of the nutrition bars that afternoon, there was only one left. Zoe broke it into pieces and passed them one at a time to the little girl.

"Chew them really well," she told her.

When there were just a couple of pieces left, she closed the wrapper. "Let's save those for breakfast. How about an apple for dessert?"

As she handed it to Becky, the little girl's eyes lit up like she'd been given the key to a candy store. Hungrily, she chomped into it and slurped the juicy flesh. When she was done, Zoe opened the other water bottle and gave her one last gulp of water.

"Now," she said, "it's time for bed."

Zoe led her to the bed we'd made and helped her onto it. She curled up into a ball and was asleep in seconds.

I looked around. Everything was in shadow. As the light faded, the forest seemed spookier.

"It's getting dark." Zoe said what I was thinking. "Do you think Dad and the searchers are still looking for Becky — and us?"

I shook my head. "If they are, they won't be for much longer. Not in the dark."

10

And Then It Was Night

Zoe and I dragged some fir boughs to the centre of the clearing and sat down back to back. She looked one direction and I looked the other, both of us straining our eyes for any movement and our ears for any sound.

My imagination was going crazy. It was like I could make things move just by thinking they were moving — even the trees. They might have been rooted to the ground for hundreds of years, but I could have sworn they were walking right toward Zoe and me.

With all my might, I willed the search party to appear. But it didn't, and after a while darkness blurred everything together.

Hope sank like a rock to the bottom of my stomach. No one was coming.

I looked up. The sky was still lighter than the trees, but not by much. I could see the shapes of things but the edges were smudged and the color was gone. There were just different shades of black. Soon they'd all be the same, and it wouldn't matter if my eyes were open or closed.

In Victoria, it never gets totally dark — not like it does in the forest. There is always something to brighten it up — streetlights, car lights, neon signs, house lights. But in the forest there's nothing except the stars and the moon.

I looked up at the sky again. There was no moon — no stars, either. Just dirty, wadded clouds.

The breeze was picking up, ruffling tree boughs and rustling leaves.

"Can you smell the rain?" Zoe asked.

"Yeah. It's getting close." I stood up.

"Where are you going?"

"To get the flashlight." I walked over to where we'd stowed our packs under the cedar tree. When I'd found the light, I switched it on and headed back.

For what seemed like an hour, Zoe and I sat in the middle of the clearing, waiting for the rain to come. For some reason holding the flashlight made me feel braver. As long as I had that teeny little light, I still had some power over the forest. But I didn't want to wear out the batteries, so I only turned it on for a couple of minutes at a time — just long enough to make sure the forest hadn't changed.

As my eyes became more useless, I heard more sounds — mostly tree toads, crickets, and birds.

"Eeeeee!" Zoe squealed suddenly and grabbed onto my arm. "What was that?"

My heart leaped into my mouth. "What was what?" I fumbled to switch on the flashlight. Then I shone the beam up and down and around.

"Didn't you feel it? Didn't you hear it?" she demanded.

"What?"

"The air around my head moved like it was being fanned, and there was a noise like wings beating."

"It was probably just the wind," I said, turning off the light and plunging us into darkness again.

"No it wasn't," Zoe insisted. "I know what wind

feels like. This was some kind of creature. It had wings."

"Well, maybe it was a bat."

"There are bats in the forest?" She pulled away and, even though it was dark, I knew she was staring at me in disbelief.

"Don't worry," I assured her. "They aren't going to turn into vampires. Your blood is safe."

There was a buzzing sound, and then Zoe slapped her cheek.

I snickered. "Well, safe from vampires anyway. Mosquitoes, maybe not so much."

A few minutes later, Zoe glommed onto my arm again and I just about jumped out of my shoes for the second time.

"What's that?"

"Zoe," I complained, "stop doing that! You're turning me into a nervous wreck!"

"I can't help it. There are eyes glowing in the dark over there."

I squinted into the night but couldn't see anything but black. "Where?"

She grabbed the flashlight, aimed it, and clicked it on. The beam reflected off a pair of shiny black eyes.

The next second they were gone.

"It's just a raccoon," I said, reclaiming the flashlight and switching it off.

For the next few minutes we were quiet. Then Zoe said, "I know we should save the food for Becky, but could we at least have a drink of water?"

"Yeah," I said. "I think we've earned it." I made another trip to the backpacks and handed Zoe the water bottle. "You first. But leave enough for me and for tomorrow morning. We're all going to be thirsty."

Zoe nodded and took a drink. Then she wiped her mouth and handed the bottle back.

I took a mouthful. The water tasted so good. I hadn't realized how thirsty I was. I wanted to gulp down the whole bottle — just like Becky had tried to do earlier.

"I bet you anything we're really close to where we need to be," Zoe said. "Like if we went ten steps in one direction, we'd see a piece of toilet paper and we'd be on our trail again and back at the bridge just like that." She snapped her fingers. "You wait and see. Tomorrow morning we're going to wake up and walk right out of this forest."

One of the good things about Zoe is that she doesn't give up. When we get to high school, I think she should be a cheerleader. Her team could be down one hundred points to zero with two minutes left in the game, and she would still be able to make the players believe they could win.

At that moment, I really needed her positive thinking. It didn't change our situation — in the morning we were going to be just as lost as we were now — but somehow, Zoe's pep talk made me less discouraged. We *would* find our way out of the forest. I didn't know how, but we would.

"The forest is kind of cool," Zoe said. "We've been so busy trying to get out of it that we haven't really noticed it."

"What do you mean?"

She took a deep breath. "Smell it. It's clean and fresh and all evergreeny."

"Evergreeny? There's no such word."

She clucked her tongue. "You know what I mean. And look at all the animals that live in the forest. Just sitting here in the dark for a few minutes, there's been a bat, birds, crickets, and a raccoon."

She paused to take a breath, and the gap she left was instantly filled with the rumble of faraway thunder. Right after that, a big fat raindrop splatted my forehead.

The forest was not only dark, it was about to get very wet. Raindrops began clattering through the trees like marbles rolling down a roof. Zoe and I jumped up, grabbed the fir boughs we'd been sitting on, and bolted for the cedar tree. Not a moment too soon, either. We barely made it to cover before the sky opened up and the rain came pouring down like a runaway river.

We huddled together under the cedar, listening to the storm crash through the trees. Clammy dampness crawled through our clothes and over our skin, making us feel as wet as if we'd been soaked by the rain itself. The forest came alive with earthy smells, and I hungrily breathed them in. I switched on the flashlight and shone it into the night. Beyond the overhang of the cedar branches, the rain was a solid sheet of water — like we were standing under a waterfall.

Then the wind picked up — blowing away from

us, thank goodness — shooting the rain toward the centre of the clearing.

I don't know how Becky slept through the storm, but she did. I guess being lost in the woods had really tired her out. Once the rain started and the wind picked up, the temperature dropped way down. Even though I had a jacket on, I could feel the cold. Becky only had a t-shirt on, but she didn't seem to feel a thing.

Zoe must have been thinking about the cold too, because she pushed past me and lay down on the makeshift bed, snuggling up as close as she could to Becky to give the little girl some of her body heat. So I curled up on the bed, too — on the other side of Becky — and covered us all with the fir boughs. Then I shut off the flashlight.

It was going to be a long night.

11

Hot Dogs for Heroes

I didn't think I would ever fall asleep — and for a long time, I didn't. It's not that I wasn't tired. I was. At least my body was. I'd been tromping through the forest all day — how could I not be tired? But my head was too full of worries to sleep.

Mostly, I was worried about finding a way out of the forest. Zoe made it sound like we were going to wake up in the morning and — just like in *The Wizard of Oz* — follow a yellow brick road right back to our campsite. Except *our* yellow brick road was pieces of toilet paper tied to bushes, and I had a feeling there might not be much of them left after the storm. Without the toilet paper trail and a compass, we could only guess the way back to the river.

That made me worry about our food and water supply. With only one apple, a couple of pieces of nutrition bar, and less than half a bottle of water left, we couldn't afford to be lost for much longer.

That gave me an idea.

I slid off the bed and felt my way to the backpacks. Then I dug around for the empty water bottle. If I propped it up in the open, it might catch the rain. Then we'd have more water. It was worth a try.

I inched toward the edge of the cedar tree umbrella and stuck my hand out. Once I could feel the rain, I knelt down and scooped a hole in the evergreen needles covering the ground. When I'd gone as far down as I could, I stuck the open bottle into the hole and built the fir needles up around it. The bottle stood up. Hopefully, it would catch some rain.

I went back to bed and listened to the storm raging around me — and worried some more. What if the storm wasn't over by morning? What if it was still pouring? Becky didn't have a jacket. Not that it would do much good if she did. Two minutes in the rain and she'd be soaked anyway. We all would. So maybe we should just stay where we were and wait for the search party. Rain or no rain, searchers would still be looking for us. Wouldn't they?

A deafening rumble of thunder cracked the night. My body jerked and my eyes flew open. Then jagged yellow lightning slashed the sky, and for a couple of seconds, the clearing was washed in a foggy blue light. It was so creepy, I almost expected aliens to come floating out of the trees. The thought made me shiver. And then suddenly it was dark again, and the rain came down harder than ever, crashing through the trees and pounding the forest floor like a drum.

I couldn't believe Zoe and Becky could sleep. It sounded like we were being attacked.

Just when I was sure it couldn't get any worse — it did.

From somewhere behind me came an enormous groan, like a giant squeaky door being pushed open. Then the groan changed to a crack that split the night just like the thunder had.

A tree was falling. It wasn't ours, but it was nearby. I don't know how I knew that, but I did. I flipped over and spread my arms across the girls. We'd all be crushed anyway, but I had to do something.

Zoe and Becky still didn't wake up. I squeezed my eyes shut and waited for the worst. Even through the downpour, I could hear branches breaking as the tree came crashing down. Then there was a thunderous boom and the ground shook.

That's when I started breathing again.

The next thing I knew, it was morning.

The day kind of snuck up on me. I could hear birds chirping, and there was a wonderful freshness in the air. It made me feel so good that for a few seconds, I thought I was back in our tent at the campsite. Then I opened my eyes and reality came flooding back. The storm was over and we were still alive, but we were also still lost.

I looked across the bed of boughs, but it was empty. I rolled over. Zoe and Becky were standing in the middle of the clearing.

"How long have you been up?" I called.

Zoe spun around and shrugged. "Long enough to go to the bathroom. I was just going to call you."

I got up and went to check out my rain catcher. The bottle was lying on its side — empty. The wind must have blown it over. So much for that plan. I sighed and shoved the bottle into my backpack.

"I'm hungry. I'm thirsty." Becky started in on her usual whining.

Zoe and I quickly pulled out the remaining food. We gave Becky what was left of the nutrition bar, but cut the apple into slices for all of us.

"Chew the pieces really well and suck out all the juice," I said. Then I doled out the water. "Just a mouthful each. We have to make this last."

"Why?" Becky frowned. "Aren't we going home now? You said we were going home in the morning."

"We are," Zoe nodded. "Right now. Right, Zach?"

"Right." I picked up my backpack and slipped it on. "So let's go."

"Which way?" Zoe asked as she put on her own pack.

I looked up into the sky. It was totally blue. The clouds were gone. I could see rays of light streaming through the trees. I pointed toward them. "The sun's there. So that's east." Then I pivoted a quarter turn right. "That means the river is this way."

Please let me be right, I prayed, leading the way out of the clearing.

As we pushed through the forest, waterlogged ferns

and bushes soaked our jeans. I didn't care. I was headed for the river, and nothing was going to stop me.

I found myself humming the song from *The Wizard of Oz*: *Follow the yellow brick road. Follow the yellow brick road. Follow, follow, follow, follow — follow the yellow brick road.*

And I was, sort of. We might not have been on a yellow brick road, but we were definitely on a path. It had to lead somewhere. My spirits picked up and I started walking faster.

"What's that?" Becky asked.

I turned to look. "What's what?"

"That." Becky pointed to a blob that looked like a soggy cocoon clinging to the branch of a bush.

I squinted at the white lump. "I don't know," I said slowly. "It sort of looks like —"

"Toilet paper!" Zoe blurted. "Zach, it's wet toilet paper. *Our* toilet paper. We tied it on yesterday. It's part of our trail! We've found our trail!"

Zoe and I started jumping up and down and laughing. For a few seconds Becky frowned at us like we'd lost our minds, but then she joined in our happy dance too.

Finally I stopped hopping around and said, "Listen."

They both froze.

"What is it?" Zoe whispered. "What do you hear?"

I grinned the biggest grin I've ever grinned in my whole life and shouted, "It's the river! And it's straight ahead of us. If we turn right, we'll be heading back to the bridge."

Then we were on the move again. When we spotted another wad of wet toilet paper, we started to jog. By the time we spotted the one after that, we were running full out and hollering at the top of our lungs.

And just like that, the bridge was straight ahead — and so was the search party, including Mom and Dad. We weren't lost anymore.

Then Becky tore past me and threw herself into the arms of some lady. "Mommy, Mommy!" I knew exactly how she felt. I was pretty happy to see my mom and dad too.

After a lot of hugging and laughing and crying and being checked over from head to toe to make sure we still had all our arms and legs, it was time to head back across the bridge. Zoe and I should have been nervous about that, but we were too happy just to be out of the forest.

Surrounded by grown-ups, we shuffled toward the river.

That's when I noticed the bridge had changed. Now a rope was strung from the tree at the end to a wooden post in the middle. It was a kind of rope handrail. Since it ran right up the centre of the bridge, we didn't have to worry about walking too close to the edge. Not that it really made a difference. With grown-ups all around us, we couldn't have fallen into the river if we'd tried. I almost laughed. It felt so good to be a kid again.

* * *

While Dad lit a fire in the concrete pit, Mom started pulling food out of the cooler — bread and peanut butter for toast, and milk for cereal. Zoe and I sat on a log, drinking water.

"Mom?"

"Mm-hmm," she said without looking at me.

"Could we have hot dogs instead of cereal?"

"Hot dogs?" she said with surprise. "For breakfast?"

"Uh-huh," I nodded. "We kinda missed supper last night."

Mom turned to Zoe. "You too?"

"Yes, please," she said.

So Mom packed away the breakfast food and handed us each a wiener and a roasting stick. Then she kneeled down and locked us in a fierce bear hug.

"Going off like that on your own was not a good thing to do," she said as she stood up again. She tried to sound gruff, but her eyes were all shiny, and I knew she was more upset than angry.

I sent Zoe my best *I-told-you-so* glare, but she ignored it and concentrated on roasting her wiener.

"We're sorry, Mom. Right, Zoe?" I said, jabbing her with my elbow.

"Ow! What did you do that for?" She poked me back. "We didn't mean to make you worry, Mom," she said. "But there was no time. The bear was right there, and Becky was so close to the river, she could've fallen in. We had to act fast."

Dad put another log on the fire. "Don't misunderstand your mother and me. We are very proud of you both. You rescued that little girl. There's no doubt about it. You just worried us, that's all."

"Sorry," I apologized again. I turned my stick and held the wiener closer to the flames. The skin bubbled and hissed.

"I'm sorry, too," Zoe said.

"The important thing is you're safe," Mom sniffed. Then she wagged a finger at us. "But don't you ever do anything like that again!"

Zoe and I shook our heads. "We won't. We promise."

Mom squirted mustard and ketchup onto a couple of hot dog buns and handed one to each of us. We slid the sizzling wieners inside, then hungrily bit into them.

"And we all lived happily ever after." Zoe grinned, her face covered in mustard. "So, what are we going to do today?"